by Jim Aylesworth | illustrated by Henry Cole

NAUGHTY LITTLE MONKEYS

PUFFIN BOOKS

To all the naughty little monkeys,
who have so enriched my life,
with love!   —J.A.

To Joan, a naughty monkey if ever
there was one!   —H.C.

PUFFIN BOOKS
Published by the Penguin Group
Penguin Young Readers Group, 345 Hudson Street, New York, New York 10014, U.S.A.
Penguin Group (Canada), 10 Alcorn Avenue, Toronto, Ontario, Canada M4V 3B2
(a division of Pearson Penguin Canada Inc.)
Penguin Books Ltd, 80 Strand, London WC2R 0RL, England
Penguin Ireland, 25 St Stephen's Green, Dublin 2, Ireland
(a division of Penguin Books Ltd)
Penguin Group (Australia), 250 Camberwell Road, Camberwell, Victoria 3124, Australia
(a division of Pearson Australia Group Pty Ltd)
Penguin Books India Pvt Ltd, 11 Community Centre, Panchsheel Park,
New Delhi - 110 017, India
Penguin Group (NZ), Cnr Airborne and Rosedale Roads, Albany, Auckland 1310,
New Zealand (a division of Pearson New Zealand Ltd)
Penguin Books (South Africa) (Pty) Ltd, 24 Sturdee Avenue, Rosebank, Johannesburg 2196, South Africa

Registered Offices: Penguin Books Ltd, 80 Strand, London WC2R 0RL, England

First published in the United States of America by Dutton Children's Books, a division of Penguin Young
Readers Group, 2003
Published by Puffin Books, a division of Penguin Young Readers Group, 2006

10

Text copyright © Jim Aylesworth, 2003
Illustrations copyright © Henry Cole, 2003

THE LIBRARY OF CONGRESS HAS CATALOGED THE DUTTON EDITION AS FOLLOWS:
Aylesworth, Jim.
Naughty little monkeys / by Jim Aylesworth; illustrated by Henry Cole.—1st ed.
p. cm.
Summary: Mom thinks all twenty-six of her monkeys are angelic, but from Andy's wayward airplane to
Zelda's trip to the zoo, these little ones find a way to get into mischief for each letter of the alphabet.
ISBN: 0-525-46940-0 (hc)
(1. Monkeys—Fiction. 2. Behavior—Fiction. 3. Stories in rhyme. 4. Alphabet.)
I. Cole, Henry, date. II. Title.
PZ8.3.A95   Nau 2003   (E)—dc21 2002040800

Puffin Books ISBN 0-14-240562-0
Manufactured in China

Naughty little monkeys
Know a lot of tricks,
But Mom thinks they're angelic,
All naughty twenty-six.

Naughty little monkey
Has a folded **airplane**.
He flies it all around
Until the rest complain.

Naughty little monkey,
Jumping on her **bed**.
It won't be too much longer
Before she bonks her head.

Naughty little monkey,
Eating chocolate **cake**.
If she eats another bite,
She'll get a tummy ache.

Naughty little monkey,
Swinging on the drape.
The curtain rod is bending
Into a funny shape.

Naughty little monkey,
Wearing Mom's **earrings**.
She's been told before
Not to touch her things.

Naughty little monkey,
Fooling with the **fish**.
All his fingers in the bowl
Going splashy, splish, splish.

Naughty little monkey,
Playing with her **gum**.
Pulling pink and gooey strings
From her teeth out to her thumb.

Naughty little monkey,
Snipping off his **hair**. . .
But he's clipped too much now—
Off to the barber's chair!

Naughty little monkey,
He's careless with **ice cream**.
The drips are dripping down
In a steady, sticky stream.

Naughty little monkey,
She's spreading grape **jelly**.
She's got it smeared all over
Her hands and chin and belly.

Naughty little monkey,
Zooming with her **kite**.
The string is getting tangled
On everything in sight.

Naughty little monkey,
Drawing with lipstick.
When his mama sees this,
It will make her feel quite sick.

Naughty little monkey
Loves his baseball **mitt**.
But playing ball indoors . . .
He really ought to quit!

Naughty little monkey,
Cutting up the **news**.
If Daddy hasn't read it,
He'll surely blow his fuse.

Naughty little monkey,
Waiting by the **oven**.
When the timer starts to ding—
Watch out! There may be shoving.

Naughty little monkey,
Stacking his **pancakes**.
All the syrup's pouring off
Into brown and gluey lakes.

Naughty little monkey,
Underneath his **quilt**.
He'll try to scare his sister
From the fort that he just built.

Naughty little monkey,
Tracking up the **rug**.
Her feet are very muddy
From some holes that she has dug.

Naughty little monkey
Goes speeding down the **slide**.
She is bound to get bruised
From such a wild ride.

Naughty little monkey,
Wearing Daddy's **ties**.
He should really know by now
That such a thing's not wise.

Naughty little monkey,
Under Mom's **umbrella**.
It's far too big and heavy
For such a little fella.

Naughty little monkey,
With a brand-new **violin**.
By now her brother's patience
Is wearing very thin.

Naughty little monkey,
Splashing soapy **water**.
This way to take a bath
Her mother never taught her.

X

Naughty little monkey,
Banging his **xylophone**.
His mom and dad are wishing
That they had not come home.

y

Naughty little monkey,
Not careful with his **yo-yo**.
Watch out for that street lamp—
Oops! Now it's an oh-no!

 Naughty little monkeys,

Heading for the **zoo**.

That's where all the monkeys go...

When the ABC's are through!